T0208390

NEXT TIME

Thomas W. Forbes

iUniverse, Inc.
New York   Bloomington

Next Time

iUniverse books may be ordered through booksellers or by contacting:

iUniverse
1663 Liberty Drive
Bloomington, IN 47403
www.iuniverse.com
1-800-Authors (1-800-288-4677)

ISBN: 978-1-4502-2680-6 (pbk)
ISBN: 978-1-4502-2681-3 (ebk)

Printed in the United States of America

Thomas W. Forbes, author

iUniverse rev. date: 10/27/2010

CONTENTS

Prologue

The guns lay silent and remained silent the entire time the young Confederate solder moved from one wounded man to another, doing so without consideration of who fought for the North or South. At one point, he received an enormous cheer from the blue and the grey. With men from both armies crying and sobbing throughout the ranks, this angel met his life's end that day. The Confederate soldier was memorialized in a statue and honored by both sides in the aftermath. I told the story as we walked up to the memorial statue.

What was odd about this was I was telling the story from three hundred yards before we could see the writing on the plague. I had never read the words on the monument honoring the confederate soldier that I had conveyed to my two friends as we walked up to the statue. They laughed and said "We thought you hadn't been here before" I answered quietly, "I haven't."

CHAPTER ONE
Enter Tom Wyatt

I entered the Marine Corps in the seventies—during the least popular war in the history of the United States. People young and old protested our presence. Patriotism was not a word associated with the Vietnam War. As a nation, it was a war fought on patriotic Premise. On a personal level, I enlisted as I had no where else to go.

It didn't take long before I was one of the wounded. In less than four months, I was out of combat, but not out of Vietnam. The morning after the fighting, I was taken from the field with two or three superficial wounds to my head and shoulder. Because of the bleeding and a deep gash that ripped across the top of my left shoulder, I was sent to the rear for medical attention.

Upon examination, I proved to be healthier than I had looked. Blood in the face and hair appears frightening even if it is not accompanied by a severe injury. And I was glad to be out of the field. I was however, a whole lot healthier than a lot of GIs in the field hospital. I was thankful that I had no serious problems and was, at least temporarily, out of the arena where such injuries could be inflicted.

As my nonlife-threatening wounds were nursed in the Saigon Naval Hospital, I fell into a one in a million opportunity. The luck came about in the form of the U.S. ambassador who was visiting the hospital on one of his goodwill, morale-building visits. He happened to sit with me that day, and the conversation turned to reassignment.

I was in no hurry to get back to the Ninth Marines, that valley, or any part of combat. My boyhood attraction with such had been altered over the past few months and, in particular, after seeing the injuries that others had suffered. Some of the guys, if they were lucky, would die. Others would return to that shit again and roll the dice one more time.

The opportunity to serve in a security position at the U.S. Embassy in Saigon was not one that I could turn down. While the threat factor around the embassy was ever increasing, the embassy was safe in comparison to an infantry battalion. I accepted the reassignment position as soon as he voiced the offer.

At nineteen, I became the youngest marine on staff and a handsome, recently wounded hero. Well, maybe not a hero, just handsome with a bit of a scar under my nose and a small one in my right eyebrow. And maybe I wasn't all that handsome, but I did have the scars and I was young. I was well received by my fellow embassy marines—all of whom had received special training in Virginia, perhaps Quantico, prior to assignment. I enjoyed the duty and became a trusted, young friend to the ambassador.

Because of that relationship, my services were often enlisted for various gray duties. Not by or at the request of the ambassador himself, but mainly by the chief of security and my fellow marines. A gray duty is simply a duty that was illegal in one way or another, yet it was a duty assigned by senior people in command.

These duties often led me into dangerous situations, placing me in parts of the city that were better not trafficked by GIs. For example, I was in charge of the morale and welfare of certain guests. That consisted of gathering ladies of the evening for these visitors and, at times, for my fellow marines—actually, the marines most of the times. I truly believe locking on hooks was much more dangerous than locking on artillery fire in combat. The city of Saigon presented its own set of dangers to GIs. There had been numerous incidents of pleasure-seeking GIs entering parts of the city and not returning.

As time would pass, I realized a certain degree of safety in maintaining relationships with certain corrupt elements of the city, not to mention serious monetary gains. Once business started, months passed without any need to cash my military paycheck. Not that military paychecks amounted to much anyway.

Business began with a trip to the hospital. This time, I drove the ambassador to the naval hospital. I was his driver 90 percent of the time. As we walked through the hospital, it was evident that it hadn't looked half as depressing two months prior. I was approached by one of the walking wounded. He questioned me concerning the acquisition of sexual pleasure on his behalf. The bottom line was he wanted female companionship—even if only for a few minutes. He knew I was from the outside. He also knew the women working in the hospital had other things on their minds, such as mending the ugly wounds left on young, American bodies.

As he spoke, my mind clicked like a cash register. Of course, I could find this brave, wounded warrior a woman. And for that matter, I could provide any of these other young patriots with the same service. After all, I had become the resident talent at the embassy for appropriating such pleasures.

Hi Lo's was one of my favorite places for gathering such ladies. Prior to my first trip to the club to do business, the guys at the embassy had told me not to give anyone my real name. Looking back, I realize how stupid I was to listen to them. The girls would return to the embassy. Within an hour, they knew everything and everyone. However, I played the game that first time I was asked my name. I was caught a bit offguard and hesitated a moment. The first name that came to mind was, Kirk, James T. I almost followed this with captain of United Federation Starship *Enterprise*.

The old gal that ran the place was a little woman with a leathery face. She took no backtalk from her girls, and they responded to her demands quickly and without questioning. She was rather like a marine drill instructor talking to a recruit. I have to say old Miss Penny and I liked each other from our first meeting. She called me her American moo-be star and greeted me by rubbing my face, at which point she would call me smooth face.. At times, she called me, jokingly of course, her little bur-gin (virgin) boy. She, of course, based the moo-be star nickname on my being such a cute, young fellow and the bur-gin on absolutely no truth at all. Heck, I wasn't a virgin and I told her that a hundred times that first night. Then again, her moo-be star talk could have been a result of old Miss Penny knowing more about the American TV adventure series than I would have thought.

The fact is that I don't know if she was pulling my leg or I was pulling hers. I must say, I did like the old gal, and the GIs liked her merchandise. At first, her girls weren't the cleanest, but they were very attractive to Americans. Miss Penny had a stockpile of sand-babies(children born of non-Vietnamese fathers) all fully grown with beautiful features—courtesy of their French fathers. They possessed round, shapely figures and sculpted facial features. They ran to me and greeted me by saying, "Oh, Jibby, we so hap' see you." It was a great time to be a young, virgin guy, although I really wasn't a virgin. Okay, so I was a virgin, but not for long.

Chapter Two
Corpsman Up

Initially, my problem was how to get these ladies into the hospital to brighten up the place. The answer came with a young corpsman named Danny Graves. He derived a plan that not only got the girls into the hospital without a problem, but he also had them checked for venereal disease prior to working for us. We did not want to start an epidemic of gonorrhea in the hospital. And there is no truth to my assisting in these examinations at any time.

Miss Penny liked the idea of the girls receiving checkups. The girls who required a shot of penicillin received it, compliments of Danny the corpsman. As an added bonus for Miss Penny, her business on the outside prospered because reports of such disease were not associated with her girls. Therefore, her establishment was not off limits for GI liberty runs.

Meanwhile, our business took off like a rocket. And speaking of rockets, Rocket was Danny's nickname, given to him by the marines on the security post. Let's just say he was fast. Danny would, at the request of Miss Penny, check all her girls monthly and, as a result of the occasional medical service provided free of charge, Miss Penny practically gave her stock to us. This made sales mostly all profit for me and Danny.

We brought the girls into the hospital by dressing them in gray, housekeeping uniforms. Ugly dresses, but the ruse worked, and we were quite the businessmen. We even made plans to bring the business home to the United States down the road. We were having a great time, a really great time. We had it all—money, ladies, laughs, and all the good times a war could give a couple of enterprising young GIs. If the war had continued for another ten years, these two patriots would have been there for the duration.

CHAPTER THREE
Tumbling Down

Things were going well; nothing could go wrong. But whoever said all good things must end was right. Everyone was happy and things were going great. In one moment, the bottom fell out without warning.

One of the girls was caught in the act by a navy commander doctor, who obviously didn't have much of a sense of humor. By his appearance and his breath, he couldn't find a whore with a hundred dollar bill pinned to his shirt collar. Anyone else would have laughed it off and let the poor GI have the round. And still, things might not have gone as bad as it did that day had the navy commander not taken her by the hand to the supervisor of the maintenance/housekeeping department, who didn't want this kind of attention following him. At this joint meeting between the housekeeping supervisor, the unauthorized visitor, and the navy commander, the names of her contacts were placed in the open.

Needless to say, business was over, and I left Vietnam faster than Robin Williams. I was personally escorted to the airport by the ambassador who told me that everything would be okay. No charges would follow, and they never did. I was, however, briefed not to mention any of the so-called gray duties for such talk would, and could, prove to be a problem for all. I not only agreed, I told him I would miss this crazy place. He wished me a good future and told me he would be seeing me again. He added that if there was anything he could do for me, just send him a letter, and he would help if he could. That was a nice thought, but I didn't see that happening. Danny Graves didn't get into much trouble either. He had a lot of insight as to the workings of the embassy at the time, so it was easier to transfer him than bring him up on charges. I never saw him again.

Chapter Four
A Time of Confusion

The Vietnam War slowly neared an end. With more than three hundred thousand members, the corps began downsizing by offering early outs. This was common in the early seventies. Separation was the word on campus, and any returnee from Vietnam got first bid nearly all the time on early outs.

I was hesitant about leaving the corps because I entered as a result of not having anyplace to go. My father had died when I was seven. My mother died a few years later, leaving me with my stepfather. I had quit high school after my junior year. It was a mistake. Yet at the time, living one more year with an abusive, alcoholic stepfather made the marines and Vietnam the lesser of two evils—and my only way out at the time.

I recall being embarrassed going to school with bruises on my face. Every couple of weeks, I had a fat lip and ran out of lies to explain them. My life was disgusting, and I needed to change it before I ended up dead or killing someone.

The entire town understood my problem. Most knew me as a good kid, even a cocaptain of the football team in my junior year. It wasn't that people enjoyed turning their heads on the subject of abuse; the world hadn't matured to that point in intervention yet. It was unheard of for outsiders to interfere with the raising of someone else's child. Visible signs of abuse did not matter. I couldn't believe my mother died and left me with him.

In desperation to get away from the abuse, I descended upon Robinson, a marine recruiter, in hopes of enlisting and being shipped out that day. I even brought my suitcase. He kind of smiled when I walked in. "You're ready, eh?"

I replied, "I'm ready, sir."

He understood. I had received a pretty good beating by the bastard the prior day. Staff Sergeant Robinson sat me down. The second thing he asked was how my face got bruised. Accustomed to lying about my bruises for so long, I told him I was bruised in football practice. He nodded his head, and I assumed he believed me because he went on with the interview. He commenced to tell me that I was too young. Funny, I hadn't told him my age yet.

He said, "What are you, fifteen, sixteen?"

I had always heard you could lie about your age and the recruiters would help you. I didn't say anything because I was sixteen.

He said, "You need to go back to school. The corps does not accept a sixteen-year-old in its ranks; there is a war going on. You need to be as far from it as you can."

I found that an odd comment for him to make to a potential recruit. I noticed he had lots of military decorations on his shirt. Later I would learn that much of it was associated with combat.

He said, "Three years from now, if you feel the same way about enlisting, come back and I'll talk more with you."

I said nothing, picked up my suitcase, and hoped no one would see me walking out. All I needed was people saying the marines had turned me down.

CHAPTER FIVE
The Visit

I had left the recruiter's office, knowing I would have to wait three more years—or just one if my stepfather would sign for me to enter at seventeen. But that same evening, we had an unexpected visitor at the house. Staff Sergeant Robinson, in uniform, came to my door, looked at me, and said, "I need to speak to your stepfather." Before my stepfather could even open his mouth, Robinson threatened to beat him to death if he put another abusive hand on the "kid." He advised my stepfather that he had killed before and doing a bastard like him in would be a pleasure. He ended by saying, "If you get brave and attempt to report this conversation, I swear I will fucking kill you."

I was sure my stepfather would turn on me as soon as Robinson left. But the coward didn't come after me that night again. A year later, without having finished school, I joined the U.S. Marines with the signature of a man who was glad to get rid of me.

CHAPTER SIX
The Return Home

Now, because of the early out, I was only nineteen. I returned home, knowing that earning a high school diploma was a priority. However, my age created a problem in my hopes of returning to the high school.

In theory, I could complete high school. However, it would have to be night school with other adults. That's not what I wanted. Heck, I wasn't that old, and I wanted badly to with some friends and in a ceremony. I went immediately to the school principal, Mr. Mallet.

Standing before him in his office in my marine uniform, I politely asked if I could return to school. First, he told me how glad he was to see me and that he and members of the school faculty had prayed for me and a good recovery from my wounds. Apparently, the local newspaper wrote some nice things in the hometown news releases based on information that the corps sent to them.

After that welcoming preamble, he sat down and advised

me that night school was the only available option. Not quite twenty and I was considered too old.

I don't know exactly what caused Mr. Mallet to change horses in midstream at that moment, but he continued, "There is a school board meeting on Friday. Tom, I won't promise you anything, but I will put your case forward and try to make an exception to the rules for you. After all, it's not like you quit because you were dropout bound. The whole town knows why you quit. Maybe, just maybe, I can get you back in."

Whatever he told them, it must have been good. That Friday night, he called me at the Martin's where I was living. The minute Mrs. Martin said, "Hello, Mr. Mallet," I held my breath as she listened to him. Smiling, she hung up the phone. At that moment, we all knew what the decision was.

Now I could finish high school the right way. Mrs. Martin said, "Tom, the local papers treated you good while you were away, and no one in this town wanted you to go. I think the decision is based on two things. One, they like you. And two, they are sorry they didn't intercede prior to your leaving."

I was back in school with one stipulation—I could not play sports, which I didn't understand at the time.

CHAPTER SEVEN
Life Was Good

School was never so good, and home life with the Martins was great as well. While I was growing up, they always cared about me and opened their door for me. Sadly, Mr. Martin had died while I was gone. He was a truly wonderful man and a father to be admired. I missed him. The family made room for me as though I was one of them. I took odd jobs trying to repay them in some way for their kindness. For a time, I was even able to draw a little unemployment.

In school, I was learning things and getting great grades. Not that I had been a bad student prior, it was just that I was better now. I think I owed those grades to a few people at that time; in particular, the school principal who stuck his neck out for me. When I really needed his help, he was there. I did notice some major differences in school. I had changed and was a bit older than most of the students, but my life had moved so radically during that time. I no longer had a lot in common with my classmates. I was older in many ways and experienced in things that I could not talk about. I absolutely stayed away from the girls that sought my attention.

One fall day, my English teacher asked the girl sitting next to me if she could babysit her young son that night. The girl had other plans. Just as the teacher turned around, I said, "I can do it."

My teacher was young and couldn't have been much more than a couple of years older than me. She asked, "Do you think you can?"

"Sure, what time should I be there?"

She said, "Seven. I'll write down the directions for you."

I walked to her home, about a six-mile walk. I was embarrassed by the fact that I had no car, but I felt I needed to contribute to my adopted family. A car would have been too much at that time, and Mrs. Martin always gave me hers if I needed it. However, on this particular night an auto priority on her part sent me walking. My teacher greeted me at the door. I was surprised to see how pretty she was with her hair down and wearing tight jeans and a sweater. She advised me that the baby, Sara, was asleep and, with a little luck, she would continue to sleep throughout the night. This was my kind of babysitting.

She said her date would arrive shortly. It had not occurred to me that she was a single mom. When he did arrive, I was disappointed—he was thin and looked like a hippie. I pictured him with his head in a bong most of his life. I couldn't believe this was a match, but it wasn't my business.

Later that evening, my thoughts concerning the two proved to be right on target. They returned after being gone for less than two hours. He offered to give me a ride home, so I grabbed my jacket, but my teacher said no, that she would take me. I couldn't help but think, *That's a crazy suggestion. The baby was sleeping, why wake her to drive me home?* The jerk didn't argue at all; he just turned and left.

She proceeded to tell me she had never gone out with him before and that it was a mistake all around. Heck, a blind man could have seen that coming. Not wanting to discuss her date, I told her the baby had slept the whole time and that I had kept going in just to see if she was breathing alright. I said that I had better get going and told her not to drive me so she didn't have to wake the baby. After all, I had walked to her home, and I could walk back. Even though it was a six–mile walk in the Connecticut cold, I was not going to let her wake the baby.

"No," she said, "it is late and dangerous."

I wanted to laugh. Dangerous? I was a marine who had just returned from war and she assumed it was too dangerous for me to walk home in this small town.

"Please, Tommy, sit down. It's not real late and I wanted to talk to you." She followed that by saying, "Tonight, all I wanted to do was get rid of this guy and get back early enough to talk with you." She told me how proud many of the teachers were of me and in particular my old football coach. I was interested in that comment and asked her how she knew that.

"I have heard him brag about you in the teachers' lounge. Just yesterday, he was saying you were made of good stuff. He said that you had suffered more than any ten kids in the school and you were making it. He also said you make everyone around you proud to know you."

"He said that?"

She smiled and said, "Every word." She paused before adding, "I wanted to talk to you many times about your returning to school and about your situation now." She told me that many people admired what I was doing and were in my corner. "Your being back in school under these circumstances is an example of your efforts and of those who want to see you succeed."

I agreed with what she said. I was sure a good many folks in our small community cheered me on from behind the scene. Heck, I couldn't pick up a bottle of milk at the store without ten people asking me how I was doing in school and what my college plans were.

As we sat on the couch, she began to question me about things she had heard concerning my life prior to entering the marines. Primarily, she asked me about losing my parents and life with my stepfather. Even though she had not been in town during that time period, I could tell she already knew the story.

She became very emotional, particularly when I pointed out that I had no place to go at the time I entered the marines. My choices were to stay at home and be abused or leave. The marines saved my life, but part of that life had to remain a secret—in particular, the lady of the evening sales program in Saigon. Most people wouldn't understand. They knew only of the young marine who was wounded in combat who had returned home and, with the help and support of his town, would attempt to start the good life!

I don't think I did a lot of leading in the conversation that night. I mostly answered questions to which she already seemed to know the answers. She did ask me about Vietnam, the night I was wounded, and specifically about the incident that got me out.

I told her that nights were always scary to me when we were not in the base camp. I explained how one night another marine and I were positioned as members of a two-person listening post. This moved us forward of the main body of troops, which made that night even more frightening.

I described how we were in the middle of the foot trail at the end of a rice paddy in the step area or levy at the end of the irrigation stair step. We had no real side depth in the fighting hole due to the water on one side and the drop on the other. The hole wasn't deep enough because of the water at the bottom of the step. But it became our listening post and our home for the evening—right smack in the center of the foot trail.

While I gave her the condensed version, the full story replayed in my mind.

*   *   *

We were on what was called a 50 percent alert, which meant one person could sleep and the other was on watch. Listening posts used radio traffic to communicate enemy movement/activity. This was the preferred method of warning the main body normally positioned fifty to seventy-five behind the listening posts. These posts were not positioned out as far as daylight defensive sighting posts because the night perimeter defenses needed to keep the listening posts in sight if at all possible. The posts had to be fixed into the night barrier plan (fields of firing, mortars, machine guns, etc.).

I don't know what woke me that night, but I looked directly down the foot trail to see three enemy soldiers. These soldiers were not regular North Vietnamese Army, but three Vietcong. The first two were armed, but I couldn't tell whether or not the third was armed as well.

Earlier that evening, we had constructed the fighting hole. The dirt coming out of the hole went into the paddy on the side. Some of the dirt was used to build a parapet, or edge, around the fighting hole. The dirt mound would not stop a bullet, but it somehow made us feel safe.

Prior to going to sleep, I had taken off my cartridge belt and placed it on top of the parapet toward the front of the hole. I also pulled out three magazines of ammo so that they were ready in case I had to reload magazines quickly. We always had plenty of ammunition and extra canteens of water. My friend and fighting hole companion that evening was sound asleep. His given name was Franklin Rossin. Some called him Freaky Frankie; but I just called him Frank.

Suddenly I awakened, the radio was leaning against his side and the enemy was thirty-five yards in front of us, coming down the walking path on a collision course with us. I was filled with panic. I had never been this close to the enemy and was unsure what to do first.

I knew I should attempt to call this in, but what if the enemy heard me talking on the radio? What if I woke Frank and he said something that would give our position away accidentally? I could try to radio click a message back, but I'd surely screw it up. Time was closing in; my indecisive ass was not moving fast enough at all.

Finally, I made the decision that we would stand a better chance if we fired first, particularly if they didn't see us. And certainly the shots would provide a warning to those in the rear. As I switched my rifle mode to fully automatic, trying to avoid the click sound it sometimes made, the first of the three soldiers walked up to the fighting hole and stopped. He stood on the parapet of the hole with my cartridge belt under his foot. Needless to say, he was surprised as he looked down.

Much less surprised, I began firing. I might not have shot at all that night had it not been for the second soldier who unslung his weapon as he walked toward the first soldier. Being together, and at such close range, they were good targets for the burst of rounds that

21

I fired. Both men fell back and went down. The first soldier was badly shot in his stomach and cried out in pain. The second soldier was killed immediately. The sounds of guns firing filled the air. Many had no idea who or what they were firing at, but their guns were adjusted to a particular field of fire. That made the experience much more frightening.

After the first shots, Frank woke up and curse words flew in rapid fire. He was scared and reacted by cursing. But as long as he was cursing, he was not dead and I was not alone. The listening post on our right, in the next lower tier of the paddy, started firing. They had visitors as well.

Frank fired down the dike, and I tried to see where the third soldier was. I was fairly sure only one was missing. I was distracted by the crying of the injured soldier in front of me; his pain bothered me greatly. Suddenly, a splashing sound came from our right front, and I was aware that someone was turning the corner on us. As I leaned forward out of the hole to look, an explosion of water, dirt, and shrapnel from a Chi-Com grenade came our way. I was in position to receive what little it did throw in our direction, and I deserved it for sticking my head out to look.

Thank God, it wasn't a U.S. grenade because it would have taken my head off at that range. In this case, fortunately for me, it was thrown into the water and mud of the rice field several meters away. All of which helped restrict the force and direction of the explosion. It did, however, catch a piece of my upper lip, side of my head, and nicked me above my eye and above the shoulder. I sustained no real damage but blood ran down my face. The wounds turned out to be relatively small, except for the one on my shoulder where shrapnel went clear across the top. I experienced little pain except for the side of my head and my mouth, which felt as though a horse had given me a quick kick right in the kisser.

Shaken up but still in the fight, I decided to use the same tactic against him, them, whatever. The enemy soldier had to be somewhere in that direction. An American grenade would be far more effective than his was. I pulled the pin and started to count it down; I didn't want this guy tossing it back at us. As I counted, Frank became worried and started yelling at me to throw it. I was nervous and didn't need his shit at the time or my concentration broken. With adrenalin pumping, I tossed it pretty good down the dike—it exploded about thirty-five meters out and off the ground. Exploding off the ground worked better for us that night. Firing was still going on; however, there was nothing in our immediate area. I decided to pull our friend in closer to us to work on him. Frank was mad and asked, "Are you crazy?"

My response was, "This one's not going to hurt us." He died before the sun came up and before any real medical attention could have been given to him. He seemed a lot more peaceful, particularly just before he died.

That morning, I was evacuated to the rear and later brought to a naval hospital. I guess they wanted to ensure the metal in the side of my head hadn't penetrated through the brain housing. My teeth were loose and my mouth hurt so I couldn't eat anything, and I couldn't afford not eating very long. I walked away from my war injuries with two, very small scars: one under my nose and one in the middle of my left eyebrow, neither were very noticeable.

* * *

By the time I had recounted my story, this very beautiful high school teacher had put her arms tightly around me. She sobbed and rocked me like a baby. I was strangely comforted by this. It was as though she was doing something I had felt her do before. I was never so calm and so comfortable with a woman than I was at this moment.

What went on from there was the most natural and wonderful moments I had ever experienced. It was a strange, different kind of pleasure with a feeling of peace afterward. It also was very warm, special, and absolutely different from that of my Miss Penny days. Everything seemed pure, as though it was meant to be and the emotion had been there longer than the hours we had spent together.

CHAPTER EIGHT
Elisabeth

Her name was Elisabeth, and she was my high school English teacher. She was twenty-five years old and beginning her second year on the job. Even though I wanted to shout about our relationship, it had to be hidden if furthered or avoided altogether. A lot was riding on this school business—not to mention our futures.

I couldn't get her off my mind. However, I knew the next day would be the determining factor. What would she say to me? Not a single word. Sitting in her class was difficult, yet I looked forward to that hour unlike no other. After that first night, I expected the next day would be difficult for her to wake up to. Two days later, she asked me to baby-sit again. She asked me in front of a couple of students, which I assumed was to avoid any raising of eyebrows should I be seen at her home.

When I got there, I realized this was not a sitting job. As a matter of fact, her mother and father had the baby for the evening. She started by saying, "I'm sorry I haven't talked to you. I'm not ashamed or embarrassed about what we shared

the other night. As a matter of fact, I keep thinking about it."
She continued by saying, "I want so much to repeat it and have
it always."

I broke in and said, "But you're not going to, are you?"

"There is too much risk in that kind of relationship between
us at this time. If people around here found out, the controversy
would destroy us both."

I could not have said it better, and she was right. I looked at
her and asked, "Obviously, you realize I have spent many hours
with thoughts focused in the same direction?"

She replied, "I imagined you had."

"I believe you're right. This will end up in tragedy if not
postponed. And on top of it all, we would end up hurting a
lot people who trust in me to make good and trust you in a
different way."

She nodded and said, "You are a wiser man than those I
have dated and, with a little education, you could go really far.
In the future, I will be there with you, if you still have feelings
for me."

All the wars in the world couldn't have stopped me from
remembering that day. You bet I could wait. And I knew the wait
was not going to be that long. In a few more months I would
be entering Bridgeport University and some serious dating with
the girl of my dreams. It was odd, the separation didn't hurt us.
This was different, so very different that she seemed to be a part
of me. I swear I could feel her soul within me. There would be
plenty of time in the future; I could hang on to that thought
for as long as it took. It was difficult not seeing her. However,
we would have an occasional babysitting night and those were
nights to remember! Graduation was right around the corner,
and I was accepted to college. Elisabeth, my pretty little angel,

was diagnosed with cancer and passed less than four months later. Our life together hadn't started when it was over. The most devastating time of my life were the weeks that led to her death. I asked myself a thousand times why her, why so young? And why is it that everything that passes through my life is attached to destruction?

CHAPTER NINE
Time of Decision

Upon her death, my life was nonexistent. However, I was sure, from that point on, that a man need not plan his future. He should just grab it as it comes. Elisabeth was an example of wasted valuable time. We could have spent many wonderful moments together, but we did not because of those around us. Worrying about what other people would think and their feelings and views. I swore I would never do such a thing again. The good things in life must be taken. I no longer had any place in my hometown. My staying could bring nothing more than memories of what was taken from me. Lost, I escaped to a familiar place: the Marine Corps.

CHAPTER TEN
Back Again

Bridgeport, Connecticut, 3:30 AM.

I sat on a curb outside a U.S. Marine recruiter's office staring down at my feet, which were encased in my old pair of marine combat boots. The rain poured and was reminiscent of a morning Vietnam downpour. A couple of hours later, the recruiter arrived. He walked toward me, looked down at me, and said, "You look like you've been here before."

I said, "Let's just do it."

I knew reenlisting in the marines wasn't the answer, but perhaps it was a window to move on, to get away. I had a strong desire to be with people who were willing to take the bull by the horns.

Corps life was new to me. It was a different Marine Corps; one I did not recognize. There was no war, and I had never been stationed at a base within the United States. I had been so young and dumb when I first entered the marines that I did not even know they had stateside assignments except for training. Upon my return, I was stationed at Camp Pendleton in California and assigned to the First Battalion, First Marines. Down the road I was reassigned to the U.S. Marine Recruit Depot in San Diego—first as a corporal drill instructor and soon, as a result of good performance, a sergeant. Shortly thereafter, I was promoted to staff sergeant.

While on the drill field, and without much thought as to my future, I made a mistake. I involved myself with a woman, which was destined to end in a failed marriage. DI duty allowed little time off. Out of a seventy-two day training schedule, I might get home twice, one day off at a time. I understand it's changed since my days and now there are four DIs to a platoon and mandatory days off every other day. Not bad, but unfortunately, that was not the case during my time. She was too young and too attractive to be trapped into my world, and I couldn't blame her.

A good attorney is a work of art. I couldn't believe how she controlled the courtroom in the midst of the divorce proceedings. She was an able speaker, and the judge listened to her every word. Yeah, she had the situation in hand. And as she spoke, I couldn't help but wish she was my attorney instead of my wife's.

That day in San Diego, the court system broke down. The justice system became unfair, and I don't think it was intentional on the part of the court system. I believe my attorney, and I might add that this was his first time up to bat, struck out miserably. He was lost in the procedures. Presenting any valuable information on my part would have been far too much for him that day. He didn't prepare for court properly and, as a result, the San Diego court system took me to the cleaners in a gross misunderstanding of military pay and allowances. This caused a large portion of my check and practically every dollar I made go towards that divorce settlement.

This left me with no options when it came to living. Even eating became a real issue. The money situation could not be corrected until my next court date, which was more than three months down the road. The divorce left me in a terrible bind. The base I was stationed at had no quarters available for what they called geographical bachelors. In turn, the corps paid me a certain allowance because of my wife support payments. But because of the allowance, I was not allowed barracks privileges and the court did not compensate for that. The entire allowance went to my ex-wife as well as a good portion of my standard pay as well.

I now had no place to live and little to live on. Jake Waters, my major at the time, helped me out. I was allowed to empty the brooms and cleaning materials from a rather large closet above the drill instructor school and turn it into a temporary room. I could fit a bed, what we called a rank, in it and a small, single-door wall locker. I needed the room, and I was thankful for it. Use of the community shower and toilet from the school completed my living arrangements. But I still needed to get the food issue turned around.

Meanwhile, I slept in a broom closet and ate items that my friends kindly brought back from the mess hall. I also ate a lot of Frosted Flakes during that period, without milk. To this day, when I see that tiger I have to smile and say, "They're GR-R-REAT!" The price was right back and the box fit perfectly on the shelf of the small wall locker. Throughout that difficult time, the major's wife, Mary, made me a tuna sandwich every day, which Jake brought to work with him.

Jake was an old corps marine. He'd been in the Korean War

as well as three tours in Vietnam. He was highly decorated with a Purple Heart that had more stars on it than Orion's belt. Each star affixed to the purple and white ribbon indicated he had been wounded. He was a marine's marine; we all loved him. He was the most respected field grade officer on that recruit depot. He and his wife took to me in a family kind of way. Jake came on hard but had a big heart. His little wife Mary worked the guy. He wasn't so hard at home. You had to love him.

CHAPTER ELEVEN
Browns

Life was not good, and I made my way to a bar in San Diego called Brown's. I had become an instructor of DIs, so I worked a regular work week. It was great. And the transfer came about during my divorce. If it had happened a few months earlier, perhaps I, or we, could have salvaged the marriage. Well, it didn't.

The bar was named after the owner, and my friend, George Harold Brown. A former marine, he was wounded in the early days of Vietnam and later became a DI as well. A friend of mine, Taylor, and I frequented Brown's place. We also wiped down the bar, served a drink here and there and enjoyed an endless supply of free draft beer for helping. Taylor and I were the only ones privileged to go behind the bar. We were also the only two broke bastards in there all the time.

Brown's beer joint was off of a recently constructed highway and smack in the middle of a lot of new industries. Overnight, this little beer joint brought in enough customers to fill the place elbow to elbow every night, not to mention a great lunch crowd. Brown served the best steak in a basket and creamed chipped beef on earth. The civilians got such a thrill out of eating chipped beef. Military personnel, active and former, couldn't understand it. Served in the mess hall, we called it shit on a shingle, among other things. Brown's really brought in a crowd, not what you would have expected by looking at the bar from the outside. For the most part, it was frequented by women and white collar workers from the new industries all around the place. And of course, there were some of Brown's kind of people—marines and DIs from the recruit depot and then only a few, because it was important to keep Brown's Bar a well-kept secret when the ladies started showing up.

CHAPTER TWELVE
Hook

My life changed overnight in Brown's place. On this particular day, the place was busy so I helped by fixing drinks for the Brown, as we called him, so he could keep up with the orders. It wasn't easy sticking those dollars in that cash register, being so poor at the time, but I couldn't do Brown that way. For that matter, I wouldn't do anyone that way.

During a lull, I sat down at the end of the bar next to Taylor. I was pretty down that day, thinking about my Corvette that was sitting on base. I couldn't drive it because I didn't have money to fill the tank or keep up its insurance as a result of my divorce. I was practically starving and life was not looking too good. Glancing down the bar, I noticed three ladies sitting together. Older gals in their midthirties, they were dressed in business clothes. Earlier, I had given one of them a beer. It was clear that their conversation was focused on us. It was apparent by the looks, the gestures, smiles, and laughter that were directed our way.

I commented to Taylor, "Hey T, I think those old gals down

there are talking about us." T, also in his midthirties, wanted to know what old gals I was referring to. He was a good guy. While in Vietnam, a machine gun barrel exploded gases in his face. Ever since, his eyes were bloodshot as though he was three sheets to the wind. T was always nervous, yet by everyone's account that knew him, he was said to be cool under fire, and I believed that. He responded to my comment by asking, "Those girls over there?"

I said, "Yeah. Hell, they're looking right at us."

T said, "Call the Brown and send him down range for a closer look."

The laughter at the other table was driving me crazy so I agreed, "Good idea. Let's send Brown to do a little recon."

Brown was like an old bull in a china shop. He walked right up to the ladies and started talking and pointing at us. He managed to embarrass two grown men! On his way back, he laughed and patted the bar every other step. Smiling like the cat that ate the mouse, he leaned over to me and said, "They're not laughing at you. The one on this end wants to buy you for the evening if you're for sale. I, of course, told her you were."

"Brown, what did you say that for?"

Meanwhile, all Taylor said, "You're shittin' me, you're shittin' me!"

I thought for a minute that it sure would be nice to drive my car again. Maybe she'd give me enough to fill the tank. Hell, I could use the money regardless of what she was spending. I told Brown I'd consider this and, by the way, how much was she willing to pay.

He replied, "A hundred dollars. How's that for your consideration?" He followed by saying, "If you do, you are hers for the evening, no questions asked. That's part of the deal."

Once again, Taylor said what he says best, "You're shittin' me."

At that point, I asked Brown if she would give me the money up front. After all, if she was disappointed, I may not get paid.

He laughed out loud so hard I thought everyone in the place was looking at us. As I reached over to cover his mouth, he opened his hand and revealed a nicely folded one hundred dollar bill. I had never seen, much less had, a hundred dollar bill. It was awesome just to look at it. Of course, my brilliant and most eloquent friend, Taylor, graced us with his repetitive mantra, "You're shittin' me."

I took the bill and asked Brown to let her know I was ready to go. T was all smiles and I was damned sure this was not happening to me. One thing I knew, I had to go through with it. On Brown's way over to inform the woman that the offer had been accepted, I heard old Brown mutter, "I'll consider this," followed by his very loud laughing. At that point, there was no turning back, I was going. It's a man thing. I remembered bringing the hooks to the embassy. Those girls were brave with never a bit of hesitation. Too bad this marine wasn't as brave as a Vietnam hooker.

She walked over and introduced herself. She then said she had to make a couple of phone calls before leaving. She smiled at her friends and walked to the phones in the rear of the bar. On her return, we left. We drove to the harbor and ate at the Embarcadero. I hadn't eaten that good in months. I ate all the bread in the basket and sent the waitress back three times to fill it up. Yeah, this woman was in the presence of a real gigolo. While I ate, I hoped she wasn't thinking that I was picking up the check. We talked. Well actually, she talked and I listened. It was a hell of a lot easier that way and it was important because the night was passing.

Evidently she thought the same thing and asked, "Are you ready? I made a reservation for us across the street." I nodded, and we proceeded to the room. It had a great view looking over the harbor, the lights, and the boats. It was beautiful but short lived as she shut the blinds. The rest of the evening went well. It was certainly okay for me, and it was the very best job I ever had.

She called me twice more that month to meet her. The first weekend of the following month, we made a trip to Big Bear. No skiing, just the view from the room. This woman was something. During our first dinner that weekend, she asked if I was interested in increasing my circle. I wondered, *What the fuck was increasing my circle all about?*

She proceeded to say she had a friend or two who would like to meet me for the same type of entertainment. *Was that what I had become, an entertainer? Look out Jerry Lewis!*

At first, I was a bit taken back. I thought she cared for me differently, but when you get down to it, business was business. The money made it such, and I never turned my hand away so I shouldn't have expected anything else.

Business grew. Through these two women, business continued to expand. I began to have a time issue. I did not have enough of it. Not everyone paid me as well. I did not ask for anything, they just paid me and I took what they gave me. But nearly everyone bought me things. Not a week would pass when a package wasn't delivered to me at work. Sometimes it was flowers, but mostly clothing. And I mean some quality type goods—not post exchange tee-shirts. My fellow marines poked a lot of fun at all this, but they were enjoying it and I was too.

Soon I did not have enough weekends or nights available. Sometimes, I'd try to set up a day to meet two, at different times of course. That was dangerous, as the wrong two could have killed me. But, what a way to go. Yes, life was good and I had a full tank all the time. I was back up to 185 pounds of good, hard stock. Being an instructor in DI school kept me in great physical condition. San Diego kept me tan and these women kept me limber and on the go. I was living in a world of exercise and pleasure, what could be better?

At that same time, I was doing what I had promised myself. I would take life on and not let it take me over. These gals took me to great places. Most of them wanted to get away from San Diego because their husbands were in the area. One client took me to the horse races over the border in Mexico. It was great; we sat in the cheap seats, enjoyed the sun, and drank cold Corona beer served with a slice of lime.

Yes, reacting to life and taking advantage of life was a good thing. One woman, in particular, gave me an education when it came to women's needs, wants, and desires. I told her she needed to put it down on paper and sell it. She would have made a fortune. I knew the information, or should I say the training, was effective, because I used everything she taught me with the others and everyone seemed very pleased with my service.

CHAPTER THIRTEEN
The Fall of Hook

A secret like mine was hard to keep among my fellow marines. There were only seven instructors in the DI school, but we were all very close. The gifts from my clients and my lack of free time to attend a fish fry with my buddies or spend ten minutes at a command function let everyone know Tommy had a busy life on the side, and they all knew what it was. The guys never tried to hurt me intentionally, but they would play with the subject matter in a joking manner frequently and in front of anyone— it did not matter. They called me the Hook. People around the base, even people I did not know, referred to me as Hook. Most did not understand the draw from that particular word.

Ultimately, the nickname cost me and stayed with me for years after. I warned the guys that they were going to get me in trouble with their joking. They continued to laugh it off. Until one, very fine day, Major Jake Waters, my officer in charge along with the DI school first sergeant and the battalion sergeant major, called me into the major's office.

I knew this summons was bad when I saw the sergeant major's face. He stood silently long and just enough to make me uncomfortable, and then the shout came, "Gunny, don't you know how to report?" I immediately reported in as ordered and stood at attention as Old Jake began to speak. A man of few words, the major spoke those few words loudly, very clearly, and used expressions that were familiar to his generation. He shouted the question to me, "Gunny, are you a whore?"

I was stunned. Stunned, as President Lincoln once said, like a duck knocked on the head. Speechless, all I could think of was the story about the young Confederate soldier who had to stand before the great Robert E. Lee. It seemed he had been involved in some infraction of the rules. The young soldier stood before Lee shaking like a leaf. The general said, "Calm down soldier, you'll get justice here," to which the young man replied, "Yes, sir, that's why I'm scared, general."

Well, at that, I did the only thing I could, and said the only thing I could. "No, sir."

The major immediately took control of the conversation and said, "That's damn good, Gunny, because there's a nasty rumor all over the recruit training regiment that you are." He paused before adding, "The first sergeant and the sergeant major here, and I, of course, don't believe such talk, but we had to ask the question." His underlings looked at me with smirks on their faces. Jake proceeded in a cautionary tone, "You know it's a good thing you're not a whore, because I would have pushed this right into a court-martial."

Major Waters closed by saying, "If anyone you know is or is even thinking about that kind of life, they would be very wise to get out of this whore business real fast and to stop thinking about it."

I kept my mouth shut. At that point, I just waited to be dismissed.

The joking stopped; the guys realized this could have cost me. As far as business was concerned, it became invisible overnight. No one was to send me things to the DI school. And, occasionally thereafter, I spent more than ten minutes at a fish fry. But mainly, I never spoke a word about any of it in front of any of my friends again. But the business didn't stop until I was transferred. This source of income was not easily given up. I liked the life and the attention.

When I was transferred, it was for a good tour of duty off the drill field. That was followed by a trip overseas and a selection into the officer rank. It was hard to imagine that after the shit I had been in, I was selected to become an officer and a gentleman. Well, an officer anyway. I was selected for warrant officer. At this time, I began officer training at Quantico, Virginia, and my life would explode into the most bizarre world I had ever experienced.

CHAPTER FOURTEEN
The Basic Officers' Course

Quantico, Virginia: basic officers course for warrant officers.

The school was not difficult. The platoon commanders were officers with little or no combat experience. In past tours of duty, either in training or in job performance, we had been exposed to most of the subjects that were taught. The overall class grades reflected the fact that we had arrived for training already knowing much of the information. With little study, most of the guys could move through this with good grades and great ease.

Those selected for warrant officer program came from good breeds of enlisted stock. Most were combat veterans; some had college backgrounds; others had college degrees. Overall, it was an odd group to look at in the showers. During happy hour at the bar, we talked and laughed about how we resembled a freak show in the showers. Many of the marines had been wounded in combat. Several men had missing toes or scars on their chests, backs, arms, or legs. A varied assortment of indents from shrapnel and bullets also were evident in various body parts.

The school tried to teach our group things such as etiquette. The first night at the Harkins Bar Room everyone was drinking out of a bottle. After our first etiquette class, which mentioned that gentlemen drank from glasses, we drank from glasses while in the Hawk military bar. That is until one of the guys returned from the head with a urinal deodorizer in his mouth. He was met with a resounding roar of laughter. The glasses hit the floor and the bottles took over. Yes, we were back in our element.

School brought forth some friends. The marines had wide and diverse interests. Those of similar interests were drawn to one another. I found sports, history, and, of course, women to be of interest. I was especially drawn to history concerning the Civil War. The states of Virginia, and nearby Pennsylvania, were rich with such history. They offered everything from battlefield tours to merchants selling memorabilia.

In conversation while at school, I met a couple of fellows who also shared this interest, and we decided to visit battlefields during some upcoming weekends. The first outing took us to a battlefield about twenty minutes from the school. As we drove into the park and down the dirt road that marked the edge of the battlefield, I looked out of the car's side window and my body chilled. Almost in a frenzy of chill, I felt sick. I couldn't say it out loud but I felt—no, I knew—that I had been here before. But that was impossible since I had never made my way down here before. The row of trees along this park road was the forward edge of a Confederate battlefront—the line of departure.

We left the car and walked onto the edge of the battlefield. Off in the distance, we saw a statue of a Confederate soldier on his knees giving a Union soldier a drink from his water pouch. This statue commemorated an incident that had occurred in the middle of battle. The Confederate soldier had moved from one wounded soldier to the next—Confederate and Union soldiers alike. He was called the angel of the battlefield. The battle paused during this action. The guns lay silent and remained silent the entire time the young Confederate soldier moved from one wounded man to another, doing so without consideration of who fought for the North or South. At one point, he received an enormous cheer from the blue and the grey. With men from both armies crying and sobbing throughout the ranks, this angel met his life's end that day. The Confederate soldier was memorialized in a statue and honored by both sides in the aftermath.

I told the story as we walked up to the memorial statue. What was odd about this was that I started telling it three hundred yards *before* we could see the writing on the plaque. I had never read the words on the monument honoring the young Confederate soldier. And I did not know anything about this battle from anything I had read or had been told. Yet, once we were in visible range and could read the written words, they were very much the story I had conveyed to my two friends as we walked up to the statue. They laughed and said, "We thought you hadn't been here before."

I answered quietly, "I haven't."

They dismissed my comment as if I was kidding them. As we turned to walk and continue our tour, I noticed two ragged, dirty looking Confederate soldiers in the distance watching us. I assumed they were a part of a battlefield reenactment and perhaps the first to arrive or they had something to do with the park.

45

One thing was certain—they looked real, very real. Their uniforms were not bright gray with yellow stripes, but they wore realistic, ragged, floppy hats and tattered clothing. They could almost pass for a couple of farmers with dirt gray apparel. I looked toward them and said to my buddies, "I wonder what those guys are doing."

They looked over to where I was glancing and said, "Who?" followed by, "What the hell are you talking about?"

Tim said, "You know, you're beginning to worry me. Do you know you're as white as a sheet?"

Now I could see the faces of the two men and one of them said, "It's him. It's time." He looked into the eyes of the other one and said, "He sees us." And I did.

It was disconcerting—these two men looked strangely familiar. As they came closer, I realized I had seen these men before, and I knew their names. I had been here when they died on this battlefield and so had I. *What the hell was I saying? What the hell was happening?* I was frightened and my two marine buddies looked at me oddly.

It had been our intention to sleep on the battlefield that night. My God, I couldn't have done that in a million years at that point. I was aware that Ned Phillips and Russell Scott, of the First Mississippi Volunteers stood before me talking up a storm. I acted as though I could not see or hear them. However, I heard every word. I had never been so desperate for control over a situation than at that moment in my life. Was I mad or was this somehow real? As these two Confederate men urged me to confirm that I could see them and talk to them, all I could do was to look away, ignoring what was happening and focusing my attention on my two marine buddies.

Ned yelled at Russell, saying, "He sees us and he hears us too."

I was ready to get out of there. I turned to my marine friends and said, "Let's go."

Surprisingly, they did not question or raise a stink, but nodded in agreement. As we turned, Ned sat down on the ground and cried out to me. I could feel the pain in his cry. I felt so bad that I turned and faced him and said, "I'll be back." They both sat still, as if amazed, and looked right at me, following me with their eyes. I could almost sense a peace that filled and comforted them.

Chapter Fifteen
Was That a Dream?

We walked back to the car in silence and returned to the base. Training weeks belonged to the marines, but the weekends were ours. I just knew my weekends were about to get crazy.

That first week after my strange encounter, I lay on my bed and thought about what had happened. As bizarre as it may seem, I became less afraid and actually looked forward to the weekend and, hopefully, another encounter with the two soldiers. I had also decided I would return alone. When the weekend finally arrived, I set off in my Corvette to the battlefield.

The closer I drove to the battlefield, the more out of touch I became with 1981. My thoughts were etched in a long ago time. A time that I scarcely remembered. It was before my birth and yet a time I was a part of. The more I drove, the more I became lost in a strange desire to seek knowledge of this past.

As I parked, the two soldiers seemed to burst into view. They frightened me a bit, yet something encouraged me and that was the thought that these two were my friends. I was sure of that.

Ned spoke first. "You can see us?" I nodded my head. He smiled and asked, "You can hear us?"

This time, I said out loud, "Yes."

He smiled again. He was so close that he lifted his arms as if to hug me, but I couldn't feel him, although I felt something. I sensed his physical presence, and, somehow, I felt his emotion. Russell drew up to me as well and now the two of them stood with their arms draped over me. They sobbed in a bittersweet way. I felt they had missed me. I intuitively felt how important this moment was to them. I stood with my head bowed, arms down by my side, and my two friends holding me.

I nodded my head and sat down on a log. They sat on either side of me. I told them, "I don't understand this. I can remember you and this battlefield somehow, but I can't remember anything prior. I really don't remember the events of the battle itself."

They began to speak of the battle and then said, "They buried you."

I asked, "Who?"

Russell replied, "The Yanks. You were the only one. They even spoke a prayer for you. They buried the rest of us days later, putting many of us in the same grave together." Then he added, "Of course, that really didn't matter."

While I tried to comprehend this, Ned said, "Look, they even built a monument for you. Do you remember giving those Yanks your water that day?"

I said I remember it happening, but I didn't know it was me.

Ned asked, "What can you remember?"

"Just the two of you. You were my friends, I think."

At that Ned smiled and said, "Friends? I think we were a bit more than that. You married my sister, Elisabeth. You remember her, don't you? She loved you and it was a great love. This war took it away early on." My heart fell to my feet and it was all I could do not to cry out.

Russell continued the story by saying, "You were quite the man that day. We were all proud of what you had done. We were surprised you didn't get shot in the first few minutes. Why that didn't happen was beyond all of us. The bullets flew, and you were calm as could be. You moved from one soldier to another without any concern except for comforting the wounded on both sides."

I said to them, "I don't know what I am doing here."

They both replied almost at the same time, "Your being here is the important thing at this moment."

Over the remainder of the weekend, I gathered more history from them. It was an interesting life I was hearing of—a good man's life. I think even if this wasn't true, even if I wasn't this man they spoke of, I would have wanted to be him.

As they reviewed this past life of mine, I recognized nothing. I could not associate this man of the past with my life today. Not at a quick glance anyway. The stories of battle drew slight recollection.

Maybe, however, what I was recollecting were soldiers' feelings—how they feared going into battle, how they worried about their reactions and the feelings that came with battle in the Civil War. Feelings that followed every soldier in every war.

Of one thing I was certain. I was still lost in all this.

Chapter Sixteen
The Past Life

As I sat and listened to my new/old friends, I couldn't have been more content. The story was about me a hundred years ago. And it was delivered out of the mouths of two dead friends.

Apparently, Ned and I had been close, almost like brothers. We grew up together in the old South, in a place near Macomb, Mississippi. The life we led had a certain degree of purity about it. I had a real attraction to the youngest member of his family—a girl named Elisabeth. She was described as the prettiest girl in the county. Beautiful smile, dark hair, and pretty blue eyes. As he spoke of her, I couldn't help recollecting another Elisabeth in his very detailed description.

He told me his sister was in love with me from the moment girls notice boys and that we were about as perfect as could be. It was a love described to be an everlasting one. I obviously took part in the war, but I didn't have the heart to injure others. Russell said, "In today's age, you would have been called conscientious."

Russell nodded in agreement when Ned said, "You guys had

it made. You were beginning to build your mill into a proper business, and you were eager to get home at night to a wife that couldn't wait to see you. It doesn't get any better than that."

I thought for a minute, he's right. Still, even as he spoke, I could not recognize any of the events. I tried hard to bring those visions to mind but found no success in my attempts. I also wondered how this man they described in this past life could have changed so much in this present life.

As I wondered, Ned turned and said, as if he read my mind, "You're not very different, not at all. The big difference and where most of the change occurred in this life was that lousy childhood you lived." He let that sink in for a moment before adding, "I can see right through you, Tommy, and you are the good man we described earlier."

CHAPTER SEVENTEEN
I Needed to Know More

I needed to know more, and the weekend didn't have enough hours in it. When I returned to school that following Monday, my mind was not in the right place. I went from the top 10 percent of the class into the lower 30 percent in two weeks, and I didn't much care. I went to the Quantico base library nightly to check the officer's professional education library in hopes of jarring my memory. I looked up anything I could find on the Civil War that involved the First Mississippi Volunteers.

I looked for mentions of the region they spoke of and anything about the town. I hoped my research would stimulate some thoughts of my own and bring back memories. But nothing I found lit any fires. I looked forward to returning to the battlefield and visiting with Russell and Ned.

CHAPTER EIGHTEEN
The Decision

That Friday I brought my sleeping bag to the battlefield and prepared to spend the weekend with my friends. Throughout all of this, I couldn't believe the peace I felt. These two beings were beyond anything I could ever have imagined, yet I had no fear. I felt an excitement that I had never before experienced. I wondered when I would wake up and find it all to have been a dream.

Spirits, ghosts, aberrations—I couldn't define any of these terms. But I was sure these two fit somewhere in the group. And that was the most interesting part of all. The fear associated with such words were absent due to the fact that I was on fire with curiosity.

Chapter Nineteen
The Thin Line

I arrived at the battlefield with my sleeping bag and two cans of soup. My Confederate friends came into view as if they had been standing next to me right along. They asked if I was planning on staying a while, and I nodded yes. They grinned and said almost in unison, "Just like old times."

I prepared my bedding and looked forward to our conversations. I wanted to talk about Elisabeth. I had to get my question answered. If she had come to me again then perhaps the future could bring it all back. And maybe, just maybe, this next time, it would last. Other curious thoughts ran through my mind, *Why? Why all this? Why this meeting? And what was to come of it all? Was it somehow accidental or was it somehow planned?* I wanted to know.

They said, "You're wondering about Elisabeth?"

I answered, "Yes." Then I followed up with, "You're reading my mind again. I am wondering about a lot of things. I am wondering what I need to do to help you two."

At that, they looked at each other and smiled. They said, "Tommy, you're not here to help us, we're here to help you."

"What? How do you intend to help me? I don't think I need your help." *And if I am the one who is in need of help, then why were they so desperate that first day, calling out to me?*

Ned answered, "I was desperate for your sake. We caused a problem in the first place. Now we must correct it for you, for us, and for everyone else involved."

Not surprisingly, I said, "I'm confused."

Ned replied, "I know you are. Let's start by saying we have been with you all through this life of yours."

I interrupted and said, "How can that be? You can't leave this battlefield." They looked at each other again and smiled and wanted to know who had told me that.

"Well, I just assumed because you're always here. This is where I see and hear you."

Russell said, "That's right, you see and hear us only here. That is because this is the last place our living souls were together united. And as a result, this ground, this place is the only place the two of us can talk to you in this life of yours. And, in reference to the battlefield, there is only a certain area where we can be together."

Ned pointed and said, "You died over there. Russell and I died over here not too far from each other. No, Tom, we don't stay here. Like Russell said, we have been around you all during this life of yours."

Ned paused, as if to let Tom take this in, before he continued. "We watched you enter this world. We were there when you were beaten by your stepfather; we went to war with you. And it was our actions there that caused the problem and is the main reason for all of this taking place. We unknowingly

56

altered history through you, and we have to turn it around with your help." He further explained, "Not everyone's life or death impacts a nation or a world's history. Some die—you might say out of a planned sequence. Others, however, cross. We made a mistake a few years ago. We are back here with you now to see if we can correct it by working together."

"What mistake?"

In unison they said, "Tommy, you both should have died that night within moments of each other."

"What night?" I asked. "What are you talking about?"

"That night in the Asian war. You tell everyone how you just woke up that night, you couldn't figure it out, no sounds, no light—you just woke up. Do you know what I am talking about now?"

"Yes. *How could I forget it?* "It was like a chill, like something was there."

Ned continued, "Close your eyes and be still."

I did so and began to feel a chill, the same chill that I felt when these two hugged me the first day. It also felt like the chill I experienced that woke me on September 11, 1970, at 3:11 am while I slept in a fighting hole attached to First Battalion Ninth Marines, Ah Sha Valley, Vietnam.

"So, you woke me, and I'm alive as a result. That's great! What is so bad about that?"

"We had no intention of waking you. We had no idea you would be able to sense our presence. We were there only to comfort you and to be with you as you opened your eyes to the next time."

"The next time? Do you want to explain what the next time is?"

"No, we have already done enough damage. We need to

correct the 'now' so the 'next' can properly come about. We have talked enough for now; let's discuss it more tomorrow after you have rested."

CHAPTER TWENTY
This Is Crazy

"How can saving my life affect this nation? I am a nobody—a U.S. Marine. Even Eleanor Roosevelt said, the marines are just oversexed, underpaid professional killers."

Russell turned and said, "Tom, listen to how you speak. You are not that person and it bothers me to hear you talk that way."

I turned toward him and said, "Maybe I feel badly that you two so strongly feel that saving my life was such a bad thing."

Russell replied, "You don't understand, it's not the saving of your life. Heck, we jumped for joy when you woke up. But that's because we weren't looking down the road and we really didn't know at that moment we had awakened you in your present life. We thought at the time you were with us. We sure didn't realize the damage we had done or how to fix it.

"I still don't see how saving my life could impact anything nationally. My God, I'm a nobody."

"Tom, it's already impacted you and the people who care for you. You want to talk about Elisabeth, let's talk. Let's answer the real question on your mind. Is she the same one? Yes, she was the person you married in 1863 and the one you lost as a result of cancer in Connecticut in 1973. You need to realize her early death was because of you."

I lashed back and yelled, "Don't you tell me that!"

He kept talking, "Tom, had Elisabeth kept on living, you would not have left Connecticut. You would have lived a very happy, successful life—a life that was meant for you and her." Russell paused to let his words sink in then continued, "The problem would have been, without her death, you would not have returned to the marines, you would never have made your way to this battlefield, and the future of millions of people would have been altered tragically."

I sobbed as he talked. I didn't care about millions of people. The fact that my life with Elisabeth was taken away because of all this angered me. I did not care about the world, just my little piece of it. And what he was telling me was that somehow it had been deliberately taken away.

Russell turned to me and said, "*Not* taken away, given. Given in hopes for your continued opportunity for happiness in the future."

"How do you guys know what I'm thinking all the time?"

He gently replied, "We just do. Tom, it's not time to be sad or mad, it's time to look forward. Look at your life today. It's not at all the embodiment of an angel of a battlefield or an angel anyplace else. Yet you certainly were such an angel here many years ago, and you will be again. Life will go on. I can't say anymore."

I faced them both and said, "I think I need to get out of here and get away from all this right now."

Ned said, "You can do as you want, but the time to prepare

for this situation is now. And remember, it is not our future, it's *yours!* We have little time to waste. We must prepare."

At that I left—angry and confused.

CHAPTER TWENTY-ONE
Ned and Russell

"How much do we tell him?"

"Enough to let his instincts lead him. Regardless of the life he has led here, he is still the same. You know that's true, Russell."

"Yes I do. But I also know that he is out of touch with much of his real spirit."

"But every time in the past, when he needed to rely on that spirit, it always came through. We saw it the night he cared for the dying soldier in that Asian war."

"Ned, he is also the guy who put the bullet in him. Our man would not have done that."

"You're wrong. Our man would have if the situation had been similar. What he did protected others, not just himself. I think he is strong—stronger than we are—and will do the right thing. Put in the right place at the correct moment in time, he will react as he must. And his actions will result in good happening. "

CHAPTER TWENTY-TWO
The Reason

At my next visit to the battlefield. it was evident that Russell and Ned were concerned about something. I thought I would lighten up the subject with a little humor.

"Okay, how do I save this world of ours?"

They both smiled. I could sense the mixture of happy and serious concern. Ned said, "You are going to prevent a mad man from assassinating a head of state."

A bit sarcastically, I said, "Oh, really. And how am I going to do this?" The conversation became quite intense, but unfortunately without any real details. A head of state wasn't good enough. "Who is this person I am to save?"

"Your president."

This was more than I could believe; it was time to leave. I'd heard all I needed at that point to realize I was delusional and imaging these two and the conversations. I was sick, sick, sick! As I got up to leave, I turned and said, "This is crazy. I would have nothing to do with such matters. How could your history put me any place near such an action or hold me responsible for the death of an American president? I would never think such a thought." I walked a few steps away before turning and adding, "You might also need to consider that the president of this nation has real security. It's not like it was in Lincoln's time."

Ned interrupted and said, "Nonetheless, he will die unless you intervene."

"What makes you think I could even get near him? I guess you figure I could call the White House daily and ask for the president's itinerary? You think I could just follow him around and try to be there when I am needed? And what about my job in the marines? I guess I could just drop by the commander's office and tell him I'll be on special assignment to save the president for the next, I don't know—how many—years."

Ned said, "Listen to these words you use."

"Never mind how I talk. This is crazy! And I couldn't be the reason a U.S. president gets assassinated. Don't tell me that." I started to walk off and turned toward them again and said, "I am sorry, but this cockamamie thought of yours is too bizarre to be real."

Russell spoke out, "And we're not? You're talking to us, that's not bizarre to you?"

He had a point. I said, "I'm sorry, I wish I could get you out of here but I can't help you, I can't do this."

Ned said, "Tom, we're not stranded here, and we don't have to be here. This is for you, for your future, and for the future of many others in this world. This is about helping you, not you helping us. I think we have said that before."

I sighed and said, "Okay, let me hear how we are to pull this off."

Ned said, "Not us, *you!*"

CHAPTER TWENTY-THREE
The Plan

The next words out of Ned's mouth were, "You can do it; you have to. We know the time and the place. All you have to do is prevent it."

I grimaced. "Is that all?"

"Look, we can practically pinpoint the location where he is shot and the time. That is pretty good information wouldn't you say? We also know it will be a gunman coming through the crowd of people at the airport. Therefore, the gunman is going to be just a few feet away when he shoots. You should be able to see him coming and stop it from happening."

"Tell me how I get a gun that close to the president without the Secret Service metal detecting devices honing in on me, particularly that close to the tape walk?"

Ned calmly replied, "You won't need a gun. All you are going to do is warn the president at the last minute. The Secret Service have guns, they can take care of the gunman. You just have to be close enough to shout a warning or something to that effect."

I echoed, "Something to that effect."

As I thought about it, he might be right. By knowing the date, time, location, and details on the shooter, perhaps it would be possible and easier to stop the would-be assassin in time. Or, I could just shout a warning like *gun, gun—guard the president!* I understood the Secret Service personnel respond well to the word gun.

According to Ned and Russell, the assassination attempt would occur about a month after my graduation from the school for newly commissioned officers. I would receive orders to Southern California and be stationed at MCAS El Toro. That was a given. From that point, it was up to me to request a one-day pass and travel to San Diego, a two-hour drive, and save the president.

CHAPTER TWENTY-FOUR
A Commitment

"You can do this, Tommy. You have to do this."

I got to thinking about it. I'd go down in history. I'd be the man who saved the president. I might even be invited to the White House, marry a congresswoman or star in a movie about it.

As I contemplated this more seriously, I realized what I was committing myself to. I also realized Ned and Russell knew more on the subject than they were willing to give up. *What was it?* So I proceeded to ask, "Will you both be there?"

Russell said, "You bet."

I said, "Will I succeed?"

"You bet."

I could not bring myself to ask the real thought on my mind. From the looks on their faces, they were reading my thoughts again. So what the hell, I had to ask, "Am I going to make it?"

They surprised me and said, "Yes, you are."

I sighed in relief and thought, *Oh, White House, here I come.*

*   *   *

On the evening of my graduation, I returned to the battlefield for the last time. I would say goodbye to these two young men once again. I didn't know what to say; it was a difficult farewell. Kind of like Dorothy in Oz, I rationalized, however, that I could return from California, she couldn't from Kansas. I figured I'd see them again.

CHAPTER TWENTY-FIVE
The Day

One month later, I was stationed in El Toro, California. And, as Ned and Russell had predicted, the president's plane was scheduled to arrive at San Diego's airport at 2:15 pm. Airport security and local law enforcement authorities were everywhere. Men and women from various security details were identifiable by the little earphone wires.

I had arrived in uniform two hours early so I could beat the crowd. I had no gun and nothing to defend myself with or to use to protect the president. I knew, without question, that my two friends were on target with all this—just by the fact this president did fly into *this* airport on *this* day. Who could have predicted it months ago? Even the president might not have known.

According to my two friends, the president would turn and begin to make his way past the security tape as he greeted onlookers. At 2:27 pm, twelve minutes after the president de-boarded the plane, an assassination attempt would be made.

If I understood Ned and Russell correctly, I stood within

three feet of where it would take place. I stood up against the yellow tape line. I glanced at my watch; the president's plane would land any minute. I took a good look at what was happening behind me. The president's plane, Air Force One, was on its final approach. The pitch of excitement in the crowd increased.

At that moment, I knew that Ned and Russell's prescient or foresight or whatever it may be called was right on. Either I was about to save an American president or a tragedy was about to behold our nation once again. *I can do this. I have to do this.* Oddly, I was not scared. I had the advantage this day, just like in the fighting hole in Vietnam. I knew what was coming and that my interference would be a totally unexpected act to the gunman. With that information, I had the advantage. I damned sure wished, however, that I had a gun.

The president's plane taxied up. As the president made his way down the open gangway, I became a bit nervous. The rows of spectators ranged from eight to as many as twelve people deep. Cameras flashed as people tried to take photos; some jockeyed for a position for a close-up view; others wanted to touch him or his sleeve. I focused on the thought that this moment was about saving the president of the United States of America.

Doubt flooded over me. It all came down to me. Why did I think I was going to be able to stop this? He's got all these damned Secret Service and law enforcement agents, if they can't stop it, how could I? I couldn't see above the crowd. Again, I looked down at my watch. It was close, less than a minute away—if my watch was correct and synchronized with the events of the day. After all, that 2:27 time was not taken from my watch. And it didn't help that my two friends couldn't give me a description of the shooter.

It was time. I looked around while keeping the president in view out of the corner of my eye. As the president neared, I turned around. I saw the assassin. He pushed and jostled his way through person after person, shoving people aside. I turned quickly to see where the president was, and as I moved, he stood with a smile and reached out to shake a hand. I turned back toward the rushing man. I saw him clearly; he was older yet very recognizable to me—*Frankie*! The rushing maniac was Freaky Frankie.

As I spotted him, I grabbed the president's wrist with my left hand. I could clearly see the face of the assassin. All I could do was yell, "noooo!" I pulled the president with my hand, rotating him like a dancer behind me as shots fired. I was hit twice in the chest and once in my arm, falling back over the tape directly in front of the president of the United States. I was a human shield. The president and I fell together. I wasn't sure if he had been hit. I thought more than one shot had been fired. I was sure, however, about the face of the gunman. The Secret Service found their mark with the gunman, and the president was not harmed.

Ned was right. Both Frank and I should have died that night in 1970—minutes apart from one another. Considering the amount of blood all over me now, I also realized we were about to make up for cheating death that night. I knew I was leaving this world. Suddenly, I had no pain as I departed from my mortal body that lay on the ground. I watched over the aftermath with no pain whatsoever. I felt a calm and a peace.

Ned and Russell were there to greet me as they had once

tried about a decade ago. Ned's first words were, "Welcome to Kansas."

We watched the controlled flurry of the Secret Service in action. The president refused to be transported away and ordered them to help me. They quickly advised him that the man was dead. He said, "That man saved me, he protected me with his body, he gave his life to protect me. Who is he?"

A Secret Service man standing nearby said, "I don't know, sir. But today, I'd say he was your guardian angel."

I turned to Ned and said, "You knew all along who he was."

"Yes, I did.'

"And, of course, you knew this was to be my last day."

He nodded in agreement as he said, "Last day *this time*. I would have told you, but you didn't ask. And you may have chickened out."

"Damned right, I would have."

Ned laughed. "You asked if you were going to make it, and the fact is, you are very much making it. Don't you understand, Tom Wyatt, you're about to embark on another wonderful life journey. And more importantly, you left this one the way you have done before—doing good and protecting and caring for others. That's your spirit and always will be."

I suddenly realized that I had a clear memory of these two guys and our past lives together. My recall became phenomenal. I had history, lives, tales, and more importantly, I had a girl who filled my existence with happiness. I closed my eyes for a moment and concentrated my thoughts on her, envisioning her in every detail. God, everything about her was so beautiful to me—her scent, her smile, her voice.

As I closed my eyes, the thoughts of her began to overwhelm

me, becoming so powerful it was as though she was standing with me, holding me, her face touching mine. I was surrounded by silence. I knew intuitively that when I opened my eyes she would be in my arms—and she was. The three words coming from that sweet voice said it all, "I missed you." As I missed her.

Everything was right. No pain, no sorrow. The only thing I could see was her and a couple of old Civil War guys with tears in their eyes. I have a feeling this time might just be the best time.